Hi,

Sam Kerr here, captain
striker for Chelsea FC.

I am so excited to be bringing you this book series about little Sam Kerr. This series follows my story from a soccer newbie to a skilled striker.

Growing up, I faced many challenges on and off the pitch. These books will share these experiences and I can't wait to share my journey with you.

I hope you love it as much as I do!

Sam

THE FLIP OUT

SAM KERR: KICKING GOALS: THE FLIP OUT
First published in Australia in 2021 by
Simon & Schuster (Australia) Pty Limited
Suite 19A, Level 1, Building C, 450 Miller Street, Cammeray, NSW 2062

10 9 8 7 6 5 4 3 2 1

Sydney New York London Toronto New Delhi
Visit our website at www.simonandschuster.com.au

 A catalogue record for this
book is available from the
National Library of Australia

ISBN: 9781761100857

Cover design: Meng Koach
Cover and internal images: Aki Fukuoka
Photo of Sam Kerr: Football Australia
Typeset by Midland Typesetters, Australia
Printed and bound in Australia by Griffin Press

 The paper this book is printed on is certified against the
Forest Stewardship Council® Standards. Griffin Press holds
chain of custody certification SGSHK-COC-005088. FSC®
promotes environmentally responsible, socially beneficial
and economically viable management of the world's forests

KICKING GOALS

Sam Kerr and Fiona Harris
Illustrated by Aki Fukuoka

THE FLIP OUT

SIMON &
SCHUSTER

London · New York · Sydney · Toronto · New Delhi

CHAPTER ONE

THE KNIGHTS' HOME GROUND

BRUCE LEE OVAL

TUESDAY

4.36 pm

'Hey, mate, wanna come and have a kick?'

Is he talking to me?

I stop spinning the footy round in my hands and look behind me. But there's just a couple of trees and the orange brick clubhouse back there. I turn and frown at the lanky man standing a few feet away from me on the oval.

'Me?'

'Yeah, you.' He smiles, pushes his Victoria Park cap back on his head and leans over the low chain mesh fence. 'I'm the coach and we're short one player.'

Dylan is warming up with the rest of the team in the middle of the oval. He grins and gives me a thumbs up. I look back at the coach.

'Yeah, nah, I'm right thanks,' I say politely, starting to spin the footy again.

'Okay, no worries, son.'

Son?

I can't help grinning to myself. This guy thinks I'm a boy. It's a fair enough mistake to make. I live in shorts and T-shirts (there's no way you'd catch me in a dress) and have short hair. Lots of people make the same mistake. It doesn't bother me.

The coach straightens up, tips his cap at me and turns back to his team. 'Right, boys, let's do some laps!'

As the team takes off around the oval, Dylan shoots me a 'why didn't you say yes?' look. But my best friend should know exactly why I didn't join in.

Soccer just isn't my game.

I kick the footy to myself as I head home. I'm thinking back to Dylan's coach asking

me, Sam Kerr, to play soccer. *Soccer*. Ridiculous. The only reason I was anywhere near
a soccer pitch today was because Dylan
dragged me there. He's been hassling me
for ages to come and watch his Under 12s
team, the Knights, train. I only agreed to
watch him today so he'd stop banging on
about it. He's always going on and on about
how awesome soccer is, even though I've
told him a gazillion times soccer isn't as
good as AFL.

The Kerrs are an AFL family through
and through. We've been obsessed with
the game for years, going all the way
back to when my dad first came out to
Australia from India. He played in the
West Australian Football League and won

his first premiership at twenty-five, which is pretty cool.

We all barrack for the West Coast Eagles, and go to every game at their home ground, Subiaco Oval. I'm in the cheer squad, too. Standing on the fence and waving the Eagles banner is the best feeling in the world. Unfortunately, the last time the Eagles won a grand final was ten whole years ago. But now that my big brother, Daniel, is playing for them, I reckon we've got a good chance of winning the 2004 Premiership.

That's what we tell him anyway. No pressure.

Daniel is ten years older than me and as crazy about football as I am. He could name the top five goal-kickers for the season by the time he was three and slept with a footy until he was eight. Playing for the Eagles is his dream come true and we're all super proud. We've been helping him improve his skills for years. Some people might even reckon we were the reason Daniel became a professional footballer.

But I wouldn't want to brag or anything.

And if we're not at Subiaco watching the Eagles during footy season, the Kerrs can always be found at the South Freo football club, where Dad coaches the Under 15s and I play in the Under 12s. So yeah, the Kerrs are an AFL family all the way, which is why I can't even imagine playing soccer. What kind of game doesn't even let you use your hands? And soccer games have really

low scores, too. Dylan told me that sometimes a whole game can go by and no one
scores a single goal. That's kind of weird
when you think about it.

Nah, soccer definitely isn't for me.

CHAPTER TWO

EAST FREMANTLE PRIMARY SCHOOL

WEDNESDAY

9.06 am

'Psst! *Sam!*'

When I don't answer, Dylan pokes a pencil into my back.

'Ow!' I turn around in my chair and glare at him.

'Sorry.' He shrugs.

'What is it?'

I glance towards the front of the class-room where our Grade Six teacher, Mr Morton, is marking homework at his desk. Mr Morton hates it when we talk while we're doing boring history worksheets in boring history class. But Dylan obviously hasn't remembered this because he's talking in a voice that is *way* louder than a whisper. My other best friend, Indi, sits next to me and gives Dylan a dirty look, too.

'Why didn't you join in training yester-day when Ted asked you?' Dylan says.

'Ssshhhh!' I say.

I check to see if Mr Morton has heard, but he's looking down and frowning at someone's homework. It must be mine. I don't know how our teacher can't hear

Dylan when he's being so loud. That's one of the good things about having a teacher who's three hundred years old. Dodgy hearing.

I can hear Chelsea and Nikita giggling at the table behind us, but I'm ignoring them. It's something I always try to do, but I've been trying especially hard since last week, when she saw me doing backflips on the oval.

'Hey, Circus Dog!' she called out. 'Nice flips!'

'Shove it, Chelsea!' Indi called back.

Indi isn't scared of anyone, not even the biggest bully in school.

'Yeah,' Dylan said in a shaky voice. 'Why don't you rocket?!'

'*Rocket?*' Chelsea squealed. 'Good come-back, dork!' Then she and Nikita walked off, laughing.

When Indi and I asked Dylan why he chose to insult Chelsea with the name of a lettuce leaf, he went red and shook his head.

'I was trying to say "rack off," but I got nervous.'

It was embarrassing for all of us.

Dylan is pretty shy and awkward around most people except for Indi and me, his best friends. Dylan's whole family is shy. His mum and dad came out to Perth from Sudan before he was born, and he's an only child. His mum is really smiley and makes the yummiest flatbread in the world.

Dylan pokes me again. 'You should have given it a go,' he says. 'For fun!'

Indi spins around in her chair. 'Shush!'

I try to focus on my war worksheet, but it's hard. Why can't Mr Morton give us worksheets about exciting stuff, like the history of the Eagles? It could have questions like: What year were the West Coast Eagles established? (1986) and, What is the Eagles' mascot? (Australian wedge-tailed eagle.) I sigh and stare out the window at the school oval. I'd much rather be out there than stuck in this stuffy classroom.

I look at the clock on the wall and can't believe my eyes. It's only 9.15! Why is time going so slowly? I still have to wait a whole hour and a half before I can go out and kick the footy with Dylan. My Under 12s team, the Blazers, have our first training of the season after school today so I really want to practise my drop punt. Dad says my kick is pretty good but thinks I can get better. There's a long hallway in our house, and one of our favourite things to do is try to curl the footy from the lounge room all the way around into the study. It's a pretty fun game. Everyone in the family has a go, even my big sister, Maddi, who isn't as good as the rest of us.

I look out the window at the oval again and imagine myself out there now, running across the grass, bouncing the ball and booting it straight through the big sticks. Boom!

'Sam Kerr!'

Uh-oh. I forgot about the war stuff and now Mr Morton is glaring at me over his black-rimmed frames. This happens a lot.

'Daydreaming again, are we?' he growls.

'Sorry, Mr Morton.'

This is all Dylan's fault. He distracted me and made me lose focus. I try to shoot death stares at my best friend through the side of my head, but I don't think it's working.

'What about you, Mr Mawut?' Now Mr Morton is frowning at Dylan. 'Anything I can help you with?'

I sneak a look and see Dylan's neck doing its embarrassed blotchy red thing. Indi sees it, too.

'Uh, no, Mr Morton,' Dylan says.

'Okay, then,' says Mr Morton, swirling his finger in the air like he's spinning an invisible yoyo. 'Then maybe the two of you could get back to your worksheets!'

I stare at the worksheet and squint my eyes, trying really hard to concentrate. I promised Mum and Dad I'd make more of an effort with my schoolwork this year, but it's only halfway through Term One and I can already feel my good intentions slipping away . . . just like the Eagles' chances at the Premiership last year.

At least we've got art next. I like art. And our teacher, Miss Keystone, is really cool. Last week she said she had a surprise project for us to work on today. I can't wait to see what it is. I'd bet my entire Eagles trading cards collection that it will be more fun than answering questions about war.

No! Stop! I have to focus on Simpson and his donkey, not daydream about how many drop punts I can fit into thirty minutes. Which is at least 280, by the way.

CHAPTER THREE

SOUTH FREMANTLE FOOTY CLUB
WEDNESDAY
4.20 pm

The ball flies through the air straight towards me. I grab it and run. I spot Cooper a few metres to my left and deliver him the ball with a short, sweet drop punt then I run hard, following the play and catching up to Cooper, who has dodged around two opposition players, barely escaping the second tackle. Cooper kicks it high over the other players as I race towards the goal square. I leap as high as I can to take the mark when . . . CRUNCH! Lenny tackles me to the ground, and I land face-first on the grass with my nose smooshed into the dirt. I sit up to give it a gentle wiggle with my finger and I feel an explosion of pain.

'Oof!'

'Sorry, Sam!' Lenny cries, leaning over me. 'You all right?'

'Yeah, I'm fine.' I grin up at him.

Lenny suddenly looks panicked and he jumps away like I'm hot lava. 'Time out!' he shouts, raising his hands above his head in the shape of a T.

I feel a bit wobbly as I stand up, still clutching the ball to my chest. It's only our first practice match of the year but I've already kicked two goals so I'm feeling pretty chuffed with myself. Then I feel something wet trickle out of my nose and drip onto my lip. Oh, great! Now I've got a snotty nose. I swipe the back of my hand across my sore face and a long, wet streak of red appears on my skin.

Hmmm, that probably isn't a good sign.

My teammates crowd around me.

'You okay, Sammy?' Josh asks.

'Is it broken?' Riley gasps.

'Good one, Lenny!' Cooper cries. 'You nearly knocked her out!'

Poor Lenny looks like he's about to cry and I know how he feels. My nose has started throbbing so hard it feels like it's going to fall off my face.

'Sorry, Sam,' Lenny says, wringing his hands. 'I didn't think I tackled you that hard.'

'It's fine,' I say. 'I'll just be faster next time.'

Everyone laughs, including me. Then I see our coach, Joe, running towards us, and he's definitely *not* laughing. The boys take a step back to let him through.

'I'm okay, Joe!' I say quickly. 'It's just a nosebleed!'

'Let me see,' he demands. 'It could be broken.'

'It's not broken.' But I'm not as sure about that as I sound.

'Come on, let's go to the rooms,' Joe orders. 'The rest of you get in threes and run some Tap and Crumb.'

I follow Joe off the oval, holding my throbbing nose and feeling angry with myself for being so stupid. How could I have let myself get hurt at the first training? Sure, Lenny seems to have grown a metre taller since last season, along with the rest of the boys, but even if I'm now heaps shorter than them, I've always been fast.

I'll just have to be faster next time.

⚽

'What do you mean, I can't play?'

I drop the ice pack onto the table with a squishy thud and stare in disbelief at the two sad faces in front of me. Everything feels like it's moving in slow motion. After Joe realised that my nose wasn't broken, just bruised, he asked me to come into the club house for a talk with him and Dad. Dad was already here, training his team on the other oval, and ran straight over when he heard I was hurt. If I'd known they were going to tell me I couldn't play footy anymore, I'd never have come out of the bathroom. The pain in my nose is nothing compared to this.

'I'm sorry, Sam,' Dad says, putting his hand over mine. 'But you've reached an age where the boys are maturing faster than you, physically. It's just too dangerous for you to keep playing with them.'

'But that's not fair!' I shout, pulling my hand away. 'It's not my fault I'm not as big as them. It doesn't mean I'm not a good player.'

'Of course it doesn't mean that, Sam,' Joe says. 'You're a better player than most of the boys out there. Your speed and mobility are second to none. But like your dad says . . . it's not an even match physically anymore.'

'We don't want to see you get hurt,' Dad adds.

'I'll be careful. I promise!'

'It's not about you being careful, Sam,' Dad sighs. 'You're playing against boys who are much bigger and stronger than you. It's not safe.'

'It would be great if there was a girls' league,' Joe says, 'but unfortunately there isn't.'

It feels like the world has tipped on its side and I'm trying really hard to hold on. Me, a Kerr, not allowed to play footy? How could that be possible? I can see how bad Dad and Joe feel about making this decision, but I don't really care about their feelings right now. I pick up my bloody tissues and run out of the clubhouse.

CHAPTER FOUR

MY BEDROOM

WEDNESDAY

7.50 pm

My chocolate brown kelpie, Penny, is sprawled across my body and looking up at me with her soft, brown eyes. She's the smartest dog in the world, and always knows when I'm sad.

'It's not fair, Penny,' I whisper, stroking the short hairs on top of her head.

Penny yawns sympathetically and nuzzles into my tummy.

Ashley Sampi and Cathy Freeman stare down at us from the posters on my wall. My two biggest sporting heroes are probably thinking the same thing as me — the world is totally unfair and why the heck isn't there a women's football league?

Footy is a rough game, so I understand (sort of) why Dad and Joe are worried about me playing against boys who are twice as big as me, but what's a footy-loving girl like me supposed to do? Take up chess?

I don't think so.

The first time I stepped onto a footy ground I knew I belonged out there. I had just joined the Auskick Under 7s team and, as soon as I got out there, I was running, weaving around other players, handballing and kicking the ball, and it all came so naturally. Since then, I've spent hundreds of hours of my life trying to copy Ashley Sampi's sensational speckies by bouncing off our fitness ball and plucking imaginary marks from the air.

Now I'll never have my real-life moment of speckie glory.

Today, when I bolted out of the footy club, still clutching my bloody tissues, I ran all the way home. I really wanted to call Dylan and Indi, but our phone is in the middle of the house, and Mum was in the kitchen, and Maddi was watching TV in the lounge room. I was worried I'd start crying on the phone and there was no way I was gonna bawl like a baby in front of my whole family.

So I came into my bedroom and had a secret cry instead.

After dinner, Dad asked if I wanted to come and have a kick in the backyard, but I told him he was being totally insensitive to even *suggest* playing a game I've been banned from! Then I stomped off to my bedroom for another secret cry. Now here I am, staring up at Ashley and Cathy.

'Knock, knock.'

It's Mum's voice outside my bedroom.

'Sam? Can I come in?'

'Yep.' I wipe my wet face and accidentally brush my bruised nose, which releases fresh tears of pain. Great.

Mum walks in and gives me one of her 'aw, my poor Sam' faces. She sits beside me and puts her hand on my leg. 'You okay, love?'

Her voice is so kind that it's super hard not to start crying all over again.

She pulls me up and puts her arms around me, which makes the not-crying thing even harder. I bury my face into her shoulder and hold my breath to try and stop a tsunami of tears gushing from my eyes.

'It sucks, huh?' Mum says softly in my ear.

That does it. Game over. There's no way I can hold the tsunami back now.

Mum rubs my back as I begin to sob and drip epic snot bubbles onto her shoulder.

'Oh, love,' she says.

After a few minutes of embarrassing blubbering, I take a deep, shaky breath and sit back.

'Okay, now that you've got that out of your system,' Mum says, handing me a tissue, 'it's time for you to make a choice, Sam Kerr.'

'About what?' I frown. 'I don't have a choice.'

'Of course you do.' Mum smiles. 'Even if you can't change the situation, you *can* change the way you deal with it. You just need to find something else that makes you happy.'

'Footy is the only thing that makes me happy,' I say. 'I don't want to do anything else.'

'You don't know that.' Mum wipes fresh tears away with her thumb. 'You're a Kerr, and we Kerrs make our own luck. If the world gives us lemons, we make lemonade spiders.'

'I love lemonade spiders,' I say quietly.

'I know you do,' Mum says. 'Now you just have to figure out what flavour you want your new lemonade spider to be.'

CHAPTER FIVE

EAST FREMANTLE PRIMARY SCHOOL
THURSDAY
8.15 am

'I can't believe you're not allowed to play footy anymore!' Indi shrieks. 'That totally SUCKS!'

We're on our way to school and Indi is being so loud that a couple of kids across the road look over to see what all the commotion is about. Indi has always been super loud. She can't help it. She's the youngest of five kids in a big Greek family and they're all loud. When you grow up in a big family, you have to have a big voice, or no one pays any attention to you. Indi might be small, but she can shout louder than the biggest Eagles supporter.

'You're the best player on the team,' Dylan says. 'It's a travesty!'

'I don't know what that means,' Indi shouts, 'but I totally agree.'

Dylan loves using words like 'travesty'. His dad gave him a book called *Storyteller's Word a Day* for Christmas last year because he said Dylan's vocabulary was 'too limited'. Now, Dylan uses words like 'rapturous' and 'unnerving' and 'travesty', which can be kind of cool, but is sometimes just plain annoying.

Seeing how outraged my friends are for me makes me feel slightly better. But only slightly . . . like how being hit over the head with a block of wood would be only slightly less painful than a sledgehammer.

'I'm sorry, Sam,' Dylan says. 'You must be gutted.'

'Yep.' I jump off my skateboard and pick it up. 'Gutted is the perfect word, Dylan.'

He pats my back and Indi puts her arm me as we all walk into school together. I'm pretty lucky to have best friends like Dylan and Indi. The three of us have known each other since we met in the sandpit on our first day of kindergarten. We are totally different from each other, in looks and personalities, but somehow it works.

Dylan is tall with sticky-outy brown hair, copper-brown eyes, and dimples, while Indi has brown curly hair that always bounces (even when she isn't moving), blue-rimmed glasses and a small gap between her two front teeth. I'm the smallest out of the three of us. I'd love to have curly hair like Indi's but mine is brown and straight and short. Long hair just gets in the way when I'm playing sport. I'm the youngest in a big family, too (I've got two brothers and one sister), but, unlike Indi, I'm the quietest. The only time I'm loud is when I'm playing footy.

Guess I'll be quiet all the time now, I think sadly as we walk into our noisy Grade Six classroom.

Indi and I sit at our table and Mr Morton starts reading out the roll. Suddenly, I can feel a lump growing in my throat.

Oh no! I don't want to cry. Especially not in front of Mr Morton.

I quickly swallow it back down, and blink as fast as I can to get rid of the tears that are pooling in the corners of my eyes.

Indi nudges me. 'You okay?' she whispers.

I nod and force a smile, but I feel like screaming. It's so unfair. The one thing I love more than anything in the whole world has been taken away from me. And there's nothing I can do about it.

CHAPTER SIX

EAST FREMANTLE PRIMARY SCHOOL
MONDAY
1.10 pm

On Monday, I'm still feeling pretty sorry for myself. Since I received the devastating news last Wednesday, the days have all passed in a miserable blur. Nothing has been able to cheer me up. Not my friends, or my family . . . not even Penny's famous face licks have been able to make me smile.

When the bell rings for lunchtime, Indi, Dylan and I walk towards the oval to our usual spot. Dylan kicks his soccer ball along the ground as we walk. When we pass by the courts, I can see our school's netball team, the Freo Flames, training there.

'Hey, what about netball?' Indi asks. 'You were a really good Goal Attack when we played in Grade Four.'

'Yeah,' Dylan says, a hopeful smile on his face. 'You were an awesome netballer.'

I stop to consider this idea . . . until I spot Chelsea Flint warming up alongside the rest of the team.

I instantly shake my head. 'Nup. Chelsea plays netball. It's bad enough having to see her at school every day. I don't want to have to look at her on a netball court, too.'

'Yeah, good point.' Indi sighs.

'Fair enough,' Dylan agrees.

'Anyway,' I say, as we continue on to the oval, 'I like netball, but I don't *love* it. Not like AFL.'

I catch Dylan and Indi sharing a worried look with each other and I feel bad about being such a downer all the time lately. It's not really fair on them. It's true that AFL is the only sport I've ever wanted to play, and that nothing else comes close, but they're just trying to come up with ideas to make me feel better.

'Hey, Sam,' Dylan says, his voice suddenly bright. 'See if you can head this back to me!'

'I don't know how to . . .'

But Dylan has already kicked the ball in the air. It sails towards me and I instinctively leap up and head the ball back to him. The ball sails through the air in a perfect arc and Dylan heads it back to me. I catch it and beam at him.

'Yes!' Indi shouts and claps.

Dylan whoops. 'Nice one!'

'Backflip! Backflip!' Indi chants.

I take a few running steps before turning into a cartwheel, then I flip over backwards through the air.

Indi claps and hoots through her hands. 'Woo-hoo! Go, Sam!'

'Sam Kerr!'

Uh-oh.

I turn to see Mr Morton standing on the edge of the oval, glaring at me over his glasses.

'Hi, Mr Morton,' I call out in my friendliest voice. Dylan and Indi are trying not to laugh, which instantly makes a giggle start to gurgle up in my own throat.

'If you insist on doing backflips on the oval, could you at least move away from the Prep playground,' he says, nodding towards the bunch of Preppies who are all gaping at me in awe, their little jaws almost hitting the ground. 'We don't want them hurting themselves if they try to copy you.'

Even as he is saying this, I can see a couple of tiny girls trying to turn cartwheels into backflips and totally wiping out on the tan bark.

'Sorry!' I call back to him. 'We'll move to the other side of the oval.'

Dylan picks up his soccer ball and the three of us run to the opposite side of the oval, far away from small eyes.

Indi bursts out laughing as we jog across the grass. 'Your face!' she cries.

We all crack up, and it's such a good feeling. It seems like ages since I had a smile on my face.

'Hey,' Dylan says, as we sit down on one of the free benches near the fence. 'Why don't you come for a kick-to-kick with me after school?'

'I told you,' I say, unwrapping my Vegemite and cheese roll. 'I don't like soccer.'

'But how do you know if you haven't tried?' Dylan persists. 'Soccer has girls' teams, you know. Not like footy. It has a pro league for women, too.'

I stare in amazement. Soccer has girls' teams? And a women's pro league, too?

'Why don't you give it a go?' Indi shrugs. 'What have you got to lose?'

Maybe they're right. And doing that header with the ball felt kind of cool . . .

'All right,' I sigh. 'I'll come for a kick. But I won't enjoy it.'

CHAPTER SEVEN

THE KNIGHTS' HOME GROUND
MONDAY
3.48 pm

Okay, so maybe I was just a teensy, tiny bit wrong about that whole not-enjoying-it thing. Turns out soccer isn't as boring as I thought. In fact, it's pretty cool.

When we came here to the oval after school last week, Dylan told me to try and kick the ball past him into the net. He's a pretty great goalie, so it was harder than I thought, and he saved nearly all of them. But I managed to sneak one or two past him. Then we did a bit of kick-to-kick and, even though it was weird not being able to pick up the ball, I got used to it after a while.

When Dylan discovered I was ambidextrous, he was rapt.

'You can fake!'

'Huh?' I frowned.

'You can trick your opponent,' Dylan said excitedly. 'You can run at your opponent with the ball at your feet, then go left instead of right at the last moment. It's such a great skill to have for soccer, especially if they've thought you were right-footed up till then.'

I had to admit that did sound pretty cool.

Dylan kicks the ball to me now, and I stop it with my foot, then boot it high over his head.

Indi has come along to watch, even though she's spent most of the time reading her book. She glances up every now and then to shout something encouraging at me. 'Nice shank!' she yells out.

'It's called a toe punt,' Dylan corrects her.

'Whatever,' Indi says, and goes back to her book.

Indi isn't into soccer, or any sports. She's happy to listen to me and Dylan bang on about teams and ladders and high scores and best-on-ground players, but she'd rather stick drawing pins in her leg than kick a ball herself.

'Okay, I'm gonna show you how to do a keepy uppy now,' Dylan says, sticking his foot out to roll the ball back to himself. 'It's a bit precocious, but fun.'

Precocious? I'll show him precocious!

Before Dylan knows what's happening, I rush at him, flick the ball out of his way and boot it into the net behind him.

'Woo-hoo!' I cry, running in a circle and throwing in a couple of backflips.

'You should come to soccer training again tomorrow,' Dylan says. 'This time you can meet our new coach properly. Ted can be a bit grumpy, but he's awesome.

We're down a player this season so I reckon you'll get a spot on the team.'

'Yeah, right.' I laugh. 'As if he's going to let me on the team when I've never played before. I don't know any of the rules or anything.'

'So you'll learn them!'

But I'm not sure. It's fine here, mucking around with my best friend, but that's different to playing with a team I don't know, and in front of the coach, too. But to be honest, this is the happiest I've felt since . . . well, since playing AFL. I've been so caught up in playing with Dylan that I haven't even thought about how miserable I am to not be playing footy. Maybe I *could* learn a new game, with all its new rules. Maybe it's worth giving it a shot, like Indi said. And there was that whole lemonade spider chat I had with Mum . . . What if soccer is my new flavour?

For the first time in my life, I'm seriously considering playing a sport that *isn't* football. The big question now is, how do I tell my AFL-loving family?

CHAPTER EIGHT

THE KERR FAMILY HOME

MONDAY

6.50 pm

'Soccer?' Daniel frowns at me across the table. 'You're going to play *soccer*?'

'Isn't soccer a Pommy game?' my brother Levi says, shoving a big forkful of spag bol into his mouth.

'Pommy?' I frown.

'It's a slang word for English people,' Mum says. 'Soccer started in England.'

'Soccer is boring as,' Levi mumbles through a mouthful of pasta.

'Actually, pretty much everyone else in the world calls it football,' I say, 'but Aussies get it confused with AFL, so they call it soccer here.'

The table falls silent, which is a very weird thing to happen in my house at dinnertime, and five shocked faces stare back at me.

'What?' I say, blushing. 'Dylan told me.'

Actually, I learnt a lot about the game of football-slash-soccer from Dylan today. He told me all about fouls, fakes and penalty shots, and how you can use your head, chest and knees to control the ball, as well as your feet. There are heaps of rules though, which were pretty confusing, to be honest. I don't know how I'm ever going to remember them all. And I don't think my family are ready to hear about any of that stuff yet. I should probably let them get their heads around the idea of a Kerr trying out for a soccer team first.

'Yeah, well, Dylan is also the one who told you that dogs have three eyelids,' Maddi scoffs. 'So I wouldn't believe everything he tells you.'

'I think that eyelids thing is actually true,' Daniel says.

'As if,' Maddi says.

'Levi, stop feeding Penny garlic bread!'
Mum says suddenly. 'I can see you. Honestly,
it's no wonder that dog is getting fat.'

Everyone laughs. We've all been guilty
of feeding Penny scraps from the table. It's
impossible to resist her big brown eyes that
say, 'Please? Just one teensy, tiny piece?'
Every dinnertime, Penny moves around the
table, from one of us to the next, waiting
for someone to give in, which we always do.
Told you she was smart.

'Anyway, Mum,' Maddi says loudly, 'did
you decide yet if I can invite three extra
friends to my party?'

My sister is having a slumber party for
her fifteenth birthday this weekend and
it's all she can talk about. I've already

organised to stay at Indi's house. I like Maddi's friends, but they all have the worst taste in music (Christina Aguilera, ugh!) and are obsessed with make-up, shopping and boys. Maddi loves AFL as much as the rest of us, but she also loves Britney Spears, which is something we definitely do not have in common.

Mum sighs. 'Yes, you can invite three more friends.'

'How many is that now?' Dad looks terrified at the thought of his house being overtaken by teenage girls.

'Twelve,' Maddi says. 'But there's another girl I'd love to—'

'No!' Mum says firmly. 'Twelve is more than enough.'

'Right, that seals it. I'm staying at Mike's that night,' Daniel says, then turns to Levi. 'You wanna come?'

Levi nods enthusiastically. He's eighteen so the idea of a house full of screaming fifteen-year-old girls is probably his worst nightmare too.

Dad nudges Daniel. 'Can I come?'

'No way!' Mum laughs and whacks Dad on the arm. 'You're staying here to help.'

Dad groans as Mum turns back to Maddi. 'We just have to work out what colour balloons you want,' she says. 'And what games you want to play.'

Maddi squeals. 'Mum, I'm going to be fifteen, not five! I don't want balloons and party hats.'

'I didn't say a word about party hats,' Mum says. 'And for your information, Miss "I'm too cool for everything now that I'm a teenager", you had balloons and party hats for your fourteenth birthday, and I didn't hear you complaining.'

Maddi almost chokes on the garlic bread. 'I did not have party hats! As *if*!'

'You did,' Mum says firmly. 'And you played that "Watching the Detectives" game.'

'That's a famous song, you know,' Dad says, reaching for a second serve of pasta and starting to sing at the top of his voice. Daniel laughs, but Levi and Maddi both clutch their heads.

'Please don't sing, Dad,' Maddi whines. 'Especially not at my party!'

My soccer announcement has clearly been forgotten. This sort of thing happens a lot in my family. There's so many of us that as soon as a new subject comes up, everyone jumps on it like a shiny new toy.

'Anyway, I think it's fantastic that you're trying a new sport, Sam,' Mum says, as if reading my mind. 'You might just have found your new lemonade spider flavour after all.'

Levi looks thrilled. 'Did you make lemonade spiders?'

'I think it's great too, Sammy,' Dad says, ignoring Levi. 'We all know what a gun you are on the footy field, so who's to say you won't slay on the soccer pitch?'

I have to love Dad's optimism, but I'm pretty sure I won't be 'slaying' anything. Apart from Dylan I don't know any of the kids on the team and I have no idea if I'll even fit in with them. And there are all those rules I somehow have to get my head around . . .

'It's a bit weird,' Daniel says. 'A Kerr playing soccer. But, hey, weirder things have happened!'

'Weirder than that?' I say, pointing at Levi, who is squirting tomato sauce all over his pasta.

Maddi shrieks as Levi swirls the big, gooey, red mess around with his fork. 'Ewwwww! You are *definitely* not coming to my party if you're gonna do disgusting stuff like that.'

Levi gives my sister an evil grin. 'Maybe I'll stay here that night after all.'

'Don't you dare!'

As my brother and sister start arguing, I realise I'm feeling better about the idea of trying out for soccer with my family's approval. Now I just have to try not to embarrass myself at training tomorrow.

CHAPTER NINE

THE KNIGHTS' HOME GROUND

TUESDAY

3.57 pm

Okay, so this is really kind of fun, I think as I run down the pitch with the ball at my feet. I might not be able to pick the ball up like I did in AFL, but the good feelings I'm having on this field are exactly the same as the ones I have on the footy oval. I feel so light and free, the way I always do when

I play sport. I reckon it's the closest feeling to flying that I'm ever going to get.

My first training session with the Knights hasn't been as scary as I expected. Ted pairs us up to practise our short passes and then gets us to work on our 'striking' (shooting for goal). We zigzag through some cones and jump over plastic sticks as part of an obstacle course, and do laps around the oval. I haven't scored any goals or got the ball off anyone, but I'm fast and got a couple of good passes in. A few times I've gone 'offside' – whatever that means – but I don't think I've made a total fool of myself. I just hope my teammates don't think I'm a deadweight if I muck up because I don't know the rules or the positions properly yet. I've never had to worry about knowing that stuff with AFL. It feels like I was born with that knowledge in me already. But this is a whole new sport with a whole new set of rules to learn.

The guys on Dylan's team are really nice and a couple of them pass the ball to me during the match, even though it's pretty obvious I've never played before. When the training session is over, Dylan and I walk over to hear what the coach has to say about my trial session.

'Not a bad effort today, Sam!'

Ted tugs at the Victoria Park cap on his head, the same one I remember him wearing the first time I saw him. I'm starting to wonder if he ever takes it off.

'Dylan can get you sorted with a uniform and we'll see you at training next week,' he says, nodding at Dylan.

'No problem,' Dylan says happily.

'Okay, thanks, Ted,' I say, feeling excited all of a sudden. 'I'll be here.'

Ted is a bit grumpy, like Dylan said, but he seems fair, which is just how I like my coaches. He gives me a curt nod now as he starts walking towards the clubrooms. 'Good to have you on the team, son!'

I see Dylan open his mouth and I quickly elbow him in the ribs as Ted walks away.

'Ow!' Dylan cries. 'What did you do that for?'

'You were going to tell him I'm not a boy.'

'Yeah, so?' Dylan frowns.

'Well,' I say, an idea starting to form in my head, 'maybe I don't want him to know I'm a girl.'

'Why not?' Dylan says. 'Ted won't care. We were a mixed team last season. It's not like AFL where only boys play past a certain age. Soccer isn't as rough as AFL. We don't have the whole full-body tackling thing.'

'It's not that,' I say firmly. 'I just . . . I don't want Ted or the team to know. I can't risk it. What if it changes things? I've already had to stop playing AFL. I don't want to have to give up soccer, too.'

I think about that flying feeling I had a few minutes ago. And I don't want to let it go.

'I dunno,' Dylan says, his eyes darting nervously from me to the front of the clubrooms where the boys are all taking their boots off. 'How are you gonna keep something like that a secret?'

'None of them go to our school,' I say. 'So how are they going to find out?'

Dylan doesn't look convinced, but he nods anyway. 'Yeah, okay. I won't tell.'

'Ace! Thanks.'

'Hey, Sam!' Ky calls from over at the clubrooms. 'Ted's got some cold sausage rolls here if you wanna come and grab one.'

'Okay!' I call back, and start to walk towards the sausage rolls. I turn to Dylan. 'So can you explain this offside rule to me again?'

CHAPTER TEN

EAST FREMANTLE PRIMARY SCHOOL
WEDNESDAY
2.34 pm

'I saw you and Dork playing soccer at lunch-time,' Chelsea sneers. 'Since when do you know anything about soccer?'

I have to try really hard to stop myself from reaching across the table and painting Chelsea's nose bright green. It's pretty tempting when I have a wet paintbrush in my hand.

Chelsea and I have been paired up to work on our new class art project. Miss Keystone's idea is for us all to make art pieces using only recyclable materials. It's really cool, apart from my annoying partner.

Indi is working on a toilet roll bird feeder with Charlie; Dylan and Stella are making tin can wind chimes, and Chelsea and I are doing a plastic bottle cap mosaic. The picture is a frog on a lilypad. I'm painting the bottle tops green for the frog and Chelsea is painting them blue for the water. Sitting with Chelsea for a whole class is painful. I can't help thinking how good she'd look with a long green stripe right down the middle of her face.

Being quiet makes me an easy target for bullies like Chelsea, but that doesn't mean I want to hear her call my best friend names.

'His name is Dylan,' I say softly, keeping my eyes on my bottle tops.

'Ha! "Dork" suits him way better.' Chelsea shrugs and takes another bottle cap out of the box. 'And you didn't answer my question. What do you know about soccer?'

Chelsea and I have never been mates, but it's our last year of primary school so I thought that maybe – just maybe – we could try and be nice to each other. I may look like an eight-year-old but that doesn't mean I have to act like one.

It's not actually Chelsea's fault that she's a bully. Maddi told me that bullying runs in the Flint family. She knows because Chelsea's big sister, Olivia, is in her class at high school and she's a bully, and Daniel said that Chelsea's brother was a bully when he was at school, too. So when you think about it, Chelsea didn't really have a choice. It would be like if you were born into the royal family. You wouldn't *choose* to have paparazzi following you all the time. Chelsea might have wanted to be the class clown or a maths whiz, until she found out that her destiny was to be the East Fremantle Primary School's bully.

'Do you like soccer?' I ask.

Chelsea scoffs. 'No! It's stupid.'

'Have you ever played?'

'Wouldn't want to,' Chelsea says. 'My uncle coaches a local loser team and asked if I wanted to join, but I said there was no way I'd play that stupid game.'

She sounds angry, which makes me wonder if there's more to the story. Then another more worrying thought pops into my head.

'What's the name of your uncle's team?'

'The Knights or something lame like that.' Chelsea paints her cap with so much force that her fingers end up blue, too.

My heart jumps up into my throat. Ted is Chelsea's *uncle*? No way! I know he's grumpy, but he doesn't seem like a bully.

'Why would I care what the stupid team is called?' Chelsea continues. 'I told Uncle Ted he wouldn't catch me dead playing in one of their games. I don't think Uncle Ted wants girls on his team anyway.'

I stare down at the half-green bottle cap in my hand as my heart bungee-jumps all the way back down to my stomach. What if Chelsea finds out I'm on the team and tells them all that I'm a girl?

'What's wrong with you?'

I look up to find Chelsea glaring at me. She must have touched her face because there are a couple of new blue dots on her cheek.

'Nothing,' I mumble. 'I'm just trying not to get paint everywhere.'

'Whatever.' Chelsea shrugs. 'This is a dumb project anyway. I'm going to wash my hands.'

She walks over to the sinks and I quickly wave Dylan and Indi over.

Indi grins. 'Is Chelsea being a pain?'

'Yeah, but listen.' I lower my voice. 'Ted is Chelsea's uncle.'

'What?' Dylan looks horrified.

'I know!' I say.

Indi's face drops. 'But if Chelsea is Ted's niece, and she finds out you're on the team . . .'

'Exactly.'

'What?' says Dylan, a bit slower at catching on.

'Chelsea knows I'm a girl,' I say, rolling my eyes. 'Der!'

'Ohhhh, right! Don't worry,' he says. 'Chelsea hates soccer. I heard her telling Nikita during sports last week. She'll never go, so she'll never find out.'

'So explain to me again why you're pretending to be a boy?' Indi says, scratching her head with the cardboard toilet roll in her hand.

'I told you yesterday.' I sigh. 'I don't want to risk Ted not having me on the team.'

How can I explain to Indi how much playing sport means to me and how scared I am of not being able to play soccer? It was horrible when I couldn't play AFL. Now that I've found something I *might* be

able to love as much, I don't want to let it go. I can still hear Chelsea's words in my head – *Uncle Ted doesn't want girls on his team.*

My mouth starts to tremble and I turn away.

'It's okay,' says Indi quietly, patting me on the arm. 'We won't tell.'

A few hours later, I'm lying upside down in our backyard hammock with my head on the grass, wondering if I've done the right thing by fibbing to my new coach and my team, too.

'Doesn't the blood rush to your head when you do that?'

I twist around to see Maddi staring down at me.

'Yeah, it helps me think,' I say, sitting up.

Maddi frowns. 'You're weird. Mum's looking for you. She needs to know what colour soccer boots you want.'

She turns to go.

'Maddi!' I stand up so quickly that I immediately fall back into the hammock again. Turns out that lying upside down makes you dizzy, too.

She turns back. 'Yeah?'

'If I tell you something, do you promise not to tell anyone?'

Maddi's face lights up. 'Sounds juicy!'

'I'm serious,' I say. 'Do you promise?'

Maddi thinks for a moment, then nods and sits down on one of our grey metal outdoor chairs that's leaning against the fence. 'Okay, promise.'

Maddi and I might be different, but we're close and I know I can trust her. If she says she won't tell, I know she means it. So I tell her the whole story and, when I finish, she stares at me in amazement.

'But why not just tell them that you're a girl?' she asks finally.

'I just told you,' I say impatiently. 'And Chelsea said her Uncle doesn't want girls on his team!'

Maddi scoffs. 'Don't listen to Chelsea!' she cries. 'She's a bully *and* a liar!'

I shrug, still not convinced.

'Listen,' Maddi says, 'your coach and teammates can see how sporty you are and they're not going to care if you're a boy or a girl. It makes no difference. You're being ridiculous.'

'I'm not!' I say. Deep down, a part of me knows that Maddi is being the Voice of Reason, but I'm not interested in hearing reason. 'You don't understand! I don't want this chance to play soccer taken off me now. I don't want to play netball or any other sport, and if I don't have AFL or soccer, what else will I have left?'

'Well, I think you should tell them,' Maddi says, standing up to walk back inside. 'It's no big deal. Lying is worse, Sam.'

'I don't want to tell them,' I say stubbornly.

Maddi shrugs. 'Suit yourself. But you better go inside and talk to Mum about what colour soccer boots you want.'

She throws me a cheeky grin as she opens the back door. 'I'm guessing it won't be pink.'

CHAPTER ELEVEN

THE KNIGHTS' HOME GROUND
SATURDAY
3.12 pm

'Sam! Get back in position!' Ted shouts from the sideline.

I look around and realise that I'm on the wrong side of the pitch.

Oops.

I was supposed to stay on the right side, at the back, to be ready for when the ball came my way, but I ran towards it without thinking.

'Over there!' Dylan shouts, gesturing towards the opposite side of the pitch.

'Gotcha,' I call back.

My first game with the Knights isn't going very well. For me or the team.

The score is 1–0 and there are only ten minutes left in the second half so it's not looking good. I spent most of the first half running around trying to get near the ball and, when I finally did get near it, I had to force myself not to pick it up and boot it across the pitch. Now I've totally forgotten what Ted said at half-time about my position.

I feel like a clueless newbie, mainly because that's exactly what I am. It's not a very nice feeling. I still don't understand what 'offside' means, or any of the rules really. Training was totally different to being out on the field and playing against an actual team. And the boys we're playing against today aren't being as nice as the boys at training, which is fair enough.

I'm not used to feeling out of my comfort zone on a sports field. But that was when I was playing footy. Soccer is a whole different ball game. Literally! What if I never feel as comfortable playing soccer as I did when I was playing AFL?

When the whistle finally blows, I just want to sink into the cold, hard ground. Mum and Dad really wanted to come and watch my first game, but I asked them not to. I'm glad they weren't here to watch their daughter embarrass herself.

'Not bad for your first game,' Dylan says, jogging up to walk beside me.

'Don't lie,' I mutter. 'I was woeful.'

'Nah, you were okay,' Ky says, appearing on my other side. 'Shoulda seen me at my first game. I sucked.'

'Don't worry, mate,' says another boy whose name I can't remember. 'First game is always rough. There's a lot to remember.'

'Thanks,' I say, feeling a little better.

We all grab our water bottles and slurp greedily from them on the sidelines.

Ted waves us over. 'Sit down, boys.'

We plonk down on the grass and listen while he gives us feedback on the game.

Thankfully, Ted doesn't single me out for doing absolutely nothing of note on the field, but he doesn't look at me either. I think that being ignored is worse than being yelled at. I stare down at my new soccer boots. Boots that I was so proud to put on this morning, imagining myself kicking the winning goal for the team. What a joke!

But I don't want my teammates to see how upset I am. It's Maddi's slumber party tonight, so I'm going straight to Indi's after here. I'll wait until I get to Indi's before I have a good sook.

I feel a tiny bit better by the time I get to Indi's. Her mum has made her famous lamb gyros for dinner and the mouth-watering smell hits me the second I step onto the Pappas family porch.

'Come into my room,' Indi says, running out of the lounge room and pulling me down the hallway. 'George and Ari are fighting about who stole whose bike.'

I can hear Indi's brothers in the kitchen.

'Blow it out your ear, George!' Ari shouts, and it makes me smile.

I love Indi's family. If anyone can cheer me up it's the Pappas family. I love sitting at their kitchen table and listening to them argue about everything, from which local cafe makes the best coffee to which public transport route to take to the city. Once Indi's dad and brother even got into an argument about which was better, margarine or butter. I secretly thought butter was better but didn't want to be seen taking sides.

'How did you go?' Indi asks now as she perches on her bed. 'I still can't believe you wouldn't let me come and watch your first match.'

'Lucky you didn't,' I groan, flopping onto the blue beanbag in the corner of Indi's room. 'I sucked.'

Indi snorts. 'You? As if!'

'It's true!' I throw my hands up. 'I had no idea what was going on half the time.'

'Rubbish!' Indi grabs one of the dozen or so beaded cushions lying on her bed and throws it at me. 'You can't have been that bad.'

'Ask Dylan if you don't believe me,' I say, catching the cushion and twirling it around on my finger like I do with my football. 'I didn't know what I was doing out there.'

'It was your first game.' She shrugs. 'You can't expect to know all the rules straight away.'

But that was the problem. I did expect to be totally across a game that involved goals and a ball, even if it was round instead of oval-shaped.

'Hey, wanna go down to the milk bar and get an ice-cream?' Indi asks, jumping off the bed.

'Sure,' I say, happy to stop talking about how much I sucked at soccer. 'But when we get back, can we sneak into the kitchen and steal some of those breadsticks your mum always puts out with the gyros?'

Indi giggles. 'If you wanna risk your life, you go right ahead.'

CHAPTER TWELVE

Dad pokes his head into the lounge room. 'Whatcha doing?'

'Watching soccer vids,' I say.

It feels a bit weird to be watching soccer in the Kerr household, so I waited until Daniel left for training and for Levi to go to his mate's place before I put the videos on. I'd forgotten Dad didn't have training tonight.

Dad comes to sit beside me on the couch. 'Where did you get them?'

'They're Dylan's.'

When I told Dylan how embarrassed I was after the weekend's match, he just laughed and said, 'You're still getting your head around the game. Once you under-stand it better, you'll be fine.'

'That's what Indi said, too,' I'd said. 'But I don't believe it.'

'I've got a bunch of videos of soccer games. I'll drop them over after school. It's a good way to learn about the rules and stuff.'

I couldn't believe it when I saw how many he had! Dylan brought over a box so chock full of video tapes that I could barely lift it. I had no idea Dylan was such a soccer video hoarder.

The ones I like the best are of the 2002 World Cup games. My favourite player from what I've watched so far is Ronaldo from Brazil. He's amazing. And my favourite teams are Brazil, England and Nigeria. There are some serious skills going on in these games, and I have to admit that it's pretty exciting to watch. It's like nothing can happen for twenty minutes, so when someone finally does get a goal, the crowd and the players go crazy with excitement.

The best part is that I think I've finally worked out what offside is. I know it will be different when I'm actually out on the pitch and playing, but maybe I can try and visualise it after watching these tapes.

'Do you like watching soccer?' Dad asks.

'Yeah, it's okay,' I say, but it's not true. It's amazing – and I feel like an AFL traitor. 'You know I'm an AFL girl.'

Dad turns to look at me. 'Why can't you be both?'

I shrug.

'I know it's a big adjustment,' Dad says. 'And starting a new sport always has its challenges. In more ways than one.'

Dad, more than anyone, knows what he's talking about. When he first came to Australia and started playing footy, some people gave him a rough time for being the only Indian on the team. People can be really stupid sometimes.

'Listen,' Dad says, picking up the remote to pause the video just as Ronaldo is running down the pitch towards the net. 'I know there's a long history of AFL players in our family, but that's not the only sport the Kerrs have been a part of. Your mum's uncle won the 1966 Melbourne Cup, riding a horse called Galilee.'

'Mum's uncle was a jockey?'

'Yep,' Dad says. 'So you see, code-hopping runs in the family!'

'What's code-hopping?'

'When you hop from one sport to another.'

Code-hopping. I like that word. I suddenly picture myself hopping from a footy ground over to a soccer pitch and my uniform changing as I cross over. It makes me smile.

'Want to do a bit of code-hopping right now and come and have a kick of the footy with me?'

'Sure!'

I jump off the couch and follow Dad outside. At least I can still play AFL in my own backyard.

No one can ever take that away from me!

CHAPTER THIRTEEN

EAST FREMANTLE PRIMARY SCHOOL
FRIDAY
10.25 am

'Guess what Stella just told me?' Indi cries.

It's recess and Dylan and I are eating our banana (Dylan) and Vegemite Saladas (me) on the school oval in the warm sunshine. We stare up at our friend standing in front of us, who's hopping from one foot to the other with excitement.

'What?' I ask.

Indi sits down next to us and grins. 'Apparently Chelsea —'

'Sssshhhh!' I say quickly when I notice Chelsea and Nikita walking towards us.

Even from twenty metres away, I can hear Chelsea bragging to Nikita about the boat her family have just bought.

'. . . and we're taking it over to Rottnest Island on the weekend,' Chelsea says, loud enough for all three of us to hear. 'I *might* be able to take you, but I'll have to ask.'

'Oh, that would be ace!' Nikita gushes. 'Thank you.'

'I can't promise anything,' Chelsea says grandly. She stops when she notices me looking in her direction. 'What are you staring at, Kerr?'

I shrug. 'Nothing.'

'Well, stop gawking at me like a weirdo then,' Chelsea snaps. 'Why don't you go work on your circus act and do some more backflips.'

Nikita laughs. 'Yeah.'

'And why don't *you* go and take a long walk off a short pier, Chelsea!' Indi shouts.

Chelsea's face goes bright pink. 'Come on, Nik,' she growls. 'It smells like losers around here.'

They walk away, and Dylan and I turn to high-five our best friend.

Indi smiles proudly. 'My sister said that to my brother the other day. It's a winner.'

'I can't believe Chelsea's family bought a boat,' Dylan says incredulously.

'Yeah, but I wouldn't want to be stuck on a boat with Chelsea's big sister,' says Indi. 'She's mean.'

'So's Chelsea,' I say.

'Olivia is *way* meaner,' says Indi. 'I saw her yelling at Chelsea down at the shops last week, and Chelsea was crying.'

Well, this is surprising. I've never thought about Chelsea being bullied herself. And by someone in her own family. That would be awful.

'Okay, so what were you going to tell us?' Dylan asks Indi.

'Oh right! I forgot.' Indi leans in and lowers her voice. 'Stella said that Chelsea *really* wanted to join your soccer team last year, but Ted wouldn't let her because she was deliberately tripping up and pushing the other players at her trial game.'

'Get out,' Dylan gasps.

Suddenly, I remember the look on Chelsea's face when I asked her if she liked soccer in art class and how angry she sounded. It all makes sense now. It must have been pretty tough, to have your own uncle keep you off the soccer team.

'Hurry up and finish eating,' Dylan says, nudging me.

'Why?' I'm only halfway through my Saladas.

'Yeah, what's the rush?' Indi asks.

'Recess is nearly over,' Dylan says. 'We should get some soccer practice in before the bell goes. Y'know, for the game tomorrow.'

I sigh and stand up to brush crumbs off my shorts. 'Yeah, okay,' I say. 'But I don't know how much good it's gonna do me. You saw how I played last week.'

'You weren't that bad,' Dylan says. 'Anyway, there's no way you could play any worse than the team we're up against this week. They're abominable.'

'Choice word,' Indi says, nodding her approval.

'Are they really that bad?' I ask.

'Totally!' Dylan says. 'Ky said they lost their first game this year 6–0. And last year we beat them by at least three goals every time we played them.'

But cockiness always makes me nervous. 'I hope you're right,' I say, turning just in time to see Chelsea throw a Prep kid's frisbee up into a tree.

CHAPTER FOURTEEN

THE KNIGHTS' HOME GROUND
SATURDAY
2.15 pm

Oh my God! Levi is here! What the heck is he doing here?

I'm trying really hard to concentrate on the game, but all I can think about is the fact that my brother is here, watching me play my second ever game of soccer.

This is very bad for two reasons:

1. I told my family this morning *not* to come to my soccer game.
2. I still don't know what I'm doing!

The Panthers may be the worst team in the league, but none of them even come close to playing as badly as I am today. It's only fifteen minutes into the first half and I've already kicked the ball the wrong way once and copped a ball square in the face when I went in for a header. The score is 2–0 our way, thanks to an awesome goal by Archie, and a sweet scissor kick by Dylan. But not even the scoreboard can make me feel better.

And now my brother is here, watching his little sister completely embarrass herself in a game he already considers second-rate. I try to ignore him for the rest of the first half, but it's not easy.

At half-time, we gather around Ted and listen as he talks strategy and rotations. He tells me to stay in my defensive zone and I nod, but I'm distracted by the sight of Levi leaning on the nearby fence. He grins and waves, but I refuse to wave back.

I'm furious with him!

The worst part of being furious is knowing I won't play well now, even if I wanted to. I can never perform well in sport when I'm angry or upset. I wish I wasn't someone who let my feelings get in the way of my game, but it's never been any different. Whenever I've had a fight with someone in my family just before a footy match, I always play really badly. I know I'll have to learn how to snap out of it one day, but I don't think today is that day.

Just ignore Levi and focus on the game, I tell myself as we jog out to start the second half.

Ten minutes in, I finally get the chance to impress my coach, my team and my brother. The opposition have possession of the ball and are passing it back and forth down the pitch. I'm running alongside my opponent, waiting for an opportunity to get near it, when a dodgy kick puts the ball directly in my path. It's there, right in front of me!

I can feel other players coming up behind me, but I know I'm faster than all of them. I sprint towards the ball, determined to get around it and kick it back towards our goal, but just when I'm about to stick my foot out, Dylan shouts out behind me.

'Sam! Get back!'

I look over to see him waving his arms around like a maniac. There's a panicked look on his face.

'What?'

The ref blows the whistle. 'Offside!'

Oh no! I forgot about the offside rule. I've run right past the defenders, which

means the other team gets a penalty shot. I'm sure my teammates must be silently cursing me, but Dylan just smiles and gives me a thumbs up.

'Don't worry, Sam,' he calls. 'Happens to everyone.'

A Panthers player lines up his shot at goal as Ted yells from the sidelines.

'Remember your defensive line formation, Knights!' he shouts.

But it's no use. The Panthers boy launches a great shot, and it flies straight past our goalie's gloves and into the top corner of the net.

As the Panthers jump around, high-fiving each other and shouting with joy, I can't bring myself to look at Ted, my teammates or Levi. That goal was my fault and I'm so ashamed.

The rest of the game is a blur.

When the final whistle blows, the score is 3–1 our way. My teammates all slap each other's backs and cheer, but I just put my head down and walk off the pitch. When I reach the sideline, I look up to see that Levi is on the other side of the oval talking to Dylan's dad. Now there's someone much worse standing next to Ted.

It's Chelsea Flint and she's staring straight at me.

What is she doing here?

'Hey, Sam,' Ted says. 'This is my niece, Chelsea. Looks like she brought us some good luck today.'

'I know Sam, Uncle Ted,' Chelsea says, narrowing her eyes at me with a big fake smile. 'We're at school together.'

The rest of the team arrive at the sideline and everyone starts picking up their water bottles and chatting happily around me.

'Hey, bad luck with the offside, Sam,' Ky says. 'But don't stress.'

Jai nods. 'Yeah, we all got stung with that one when we started playing.'

'You're doing great,' Dylan says.

Chelsea laughs. 'Apart from when you hit the ball with your face instead of your foot.'

'Hey, come on,' Ted says, nudging

Chelsea. 'Give the kid a break. He's only played two games.'

'He?' Chelsea frowns. 'Did you just call Sam a *he*?'

Everyone immediately stops chatting.

Ted frowns. 'Yeah, why?'

'Sam's a girl!' Chelsea laughs. 'Did she tell you she was a boy? Oh, that's too funny. She's a *girl*!'

Ted's bushy, sandy-coloured eyebrows shoot up and disappear under the peak of his cap and his bright blue eyes go wide. The silence from my team is heavy.

As Chelsea stares at me, a look of pure glee on her face, my stomach plummets down into my studded, green boots.

I pick up my bag, push my way through my stunned teammates and run away from the soccer ground as fast as my sore legs will take me.

CHAPTER FIFTEEN

MY BACKYARD

SATURDAY

4.20 pm

Everything is a mess. A big fat humiliating mess.

I'm sitting in the backyard with Penny on my lap. She knows I've had the worst morning of my life so every eight seconds she gives my face a lick. She's pretty much the only good thing in my life right now.

I'm totally miserable. I miss footy so much. I miss my teammates, my club and everything about it. Soccer is dumb. I hate the stupid offside rule and the stupid penalty kicks and the stupid no-picking-up-the-ball-with-your-hands. It doesn't matter though, because I'm never going to play it again anyway. If Ted doesn't kick me off the team for lying to him, which I'm pretty sure he will, I'm going to quit.

The back door opens and Levi walks out carrying a training bag in one hand and a footy in the other.

'Wow,' he says with a grin, plonking down on the grass next to me. 'Our doorbell is working overtime today.'

'What?'

'From all the people coming to our front door,' Levi says. 'Dylan, Indi, your coach . . .'

What? Dylan came over? And Indi too? Dylan must have told her what happened, so she's come to see if I'm okay. And now I'm feeling even worse – I'm guessing Ted came over to tell me I'm off the team.

'What did you say to them?' I ask in a small voice.

'I said you needed to be on your own for a bit and sent them all away,' Levi says.

'Thanks,' I mutter. 'Even though I'm actually not talking to you.'

His eyes widen. 'What did I do?'

I do my best 'Angry Mum' impression. 'You came to my game after I told you not to!'

But Levi doesn't seem intimidated by my excellent impersonation.

'Yeah, sorry about that.' He shrugs and reaches over to give Penny a pat. 'Couldn't help it. I just had to see it for myself.'

'Well, I hope you enjoyed watching me make a total fool of myself.'

'Don't be such a drama queen.'

'I'm not!'

'You are.' He gives me a gentle shove. 'You didn't make a fool of yourself. You're learning a new game. You're fast and agile and you've got potential. That's what your coach says anyway.'

A warm feeling rushes through my body. Ted said I was agile! That I had potential! But then something else occurs to me and I stare at Levi in horror.

'You spoke to Ted?' I take a deep breath. 'So, did he tell you . . .'

'That I have two brothers now?' Levi laughs. 'Yeah, he did. You doofus! Why did you say you were a boy?'

I pull at the grass. 'Is he mad?'

'He wants you to go to training this week, so that's a good sign.'

'But why? I'm terrible.'

'You're not, you know.' Levi taps me on the forehead. 'You've just gotta change what's going on in here. It's your biggest enemy. Ted's right, you *are* agile, and I can see your potential, too. But I can see you out there getting all in your head about it and worrying about how good you are or if you suck. If you don't change your mindset, then you really *will* suck.'

'I miss footy,' I say softly.

'I know, mate,' Levi says, putting his arm around me. 'But soccer is pretty cool, too. I enjoyed watching today.'

'Are you just saying that to make me feel better?'

'No, I really did.'

I believe him, too. I know my brother pretty well and he's a terrible liar. Even Penny thumps her tail on the grass in agreement.

'Just don't tell anyone I said that,' he adds. 'I'll totally deny it if you do.'

That makes me laugh.

'Listen, Sammy,' Levi says, shuffling around so that we're sitting face to face, cross-legged on the grass. 'When successful people get knocked down, they get straight back up. They make mistakes but they don't quit. You say you want to give soccer a proper go, but that's not what you're doing, not really. You can't just expect to be good at it straight away.'

'But I have been doing extra practice,' I say. 'At school, with Dylan.'

'When you were playing footy, you never had a ball out of your hands,' Levi says. 'Now you need to do the same thing with soccer – you need to have a soccer ball at your feet all the time.'

Levi's right. It's true that I had natural skill when I was playing AFL, but I still had to practise and work hard at it when I was off the field, too. That's how I became so good at it. Now I have to do the same with soccer.

A wave of confidence washes over me as I look into my brother's face. *I can do this*. I know I can. If I really put my mind to it, I'm sure I can play soccer just as well as I played AFL.

Levi unzips his training bag and pulls out a brand-new soccer ball.

'That's why I got you this.' He throws it in the air, and I catch it. 'Now, stop sitting here feeling sorry for yourself and start practising.'

CHAPTER SIXTEEN

MY HOUSE
THE WEEKEND

So I do.

All through the rest of the weekend, my new soccer ball is hardly ever out of my sight. I kick it up and down the hallway, juggle it on my knees and try to flick it up with my foot and bounce it off my chest.

'Sam!' Mum shouts after I've been playing wall-ball in the hallway for over an hour. 'If I hear that ball thump against the wall one more time, I'm going to lose my mind. Outside!'

Then, 'I'm gonna pop that stupid ball if you don't stop!' Maddi yells, after I've spent ten minutes playing push-pull in the lounge room where she's watching TV.

Push-pull is where you move the ball back and forth from toe to heel to toe, switching feet really quickly, and I can't stop because I'm just about to hit two hundred.

Levi sticks his head into the lounge room just as Maddi jumps up from the couch and lunges for the ball. 'She's gotta practise!' he says. 'Leave her alone.'

'Does she have to practise all the time?'
Maddi huffs, but she leaves the ball alone
and sits back down with the TV volume
up loud.

All the extra work is definitely making a
difference and, by the end of the weekend,
I'm feeling way more comfortable with a
soccer ball at my feet. The only problem will
be having to face everyone at training on
Tuesday. I'm also dreading seeing Chelsea
at school on Monday.

As it turns out, I don't have to wait long.
Chelsea is leaning on the school fence when
Dylan, Indi and I walk through the gate
on Monday morning. It's like she's been
waiting for me.

'So are you a girl today, Sam?' Chelsea sneers. 'Or still a boy?'

Indi bristles, but before she can say a word, I surprise everyone, including myself, by getting in first.

'Blow it out your ear, Chelsea!' I say loudly. Then I flick my skateboard up, making her jump out of the way, and chuck it under my arm.

Chelsea stares, open-mouthed in amazement. Dylan looks even more shocked than Chelsea.

'Yes, girl!' Indi shrieks, high-fiving me.

The three of us spin on our sneakers and waltz into school, our heads held high. In the whole six years of knowing her, it's the first time I've ever stood up to Chelsea Flint and it feels good. I silently thank Ari Pappas for the inspiration.

Dylan helps me work on my soccer skills at recess and lunchtime. Even Indi puts her book down to goalie for us at one point. Now, instead of trying to replicate Ashley Sampi's speckies by bouncing off fitness balls to pluck marks from the air, I try to copy David Beckham's moves. He's a famous English midfielder who can 'bend' his free kicks, curving the ball around defenders to score. I've even put a poster of him up on my wall, right next to Cathy and Ashley, to inspire me. I spend all of Monday afternoon trying to strike the ball with the inside of my foot, leaning my body the other way to get an extra curl on the ball. It's hard, but I picture being able to do it one day and surprising Ted and the team, so I keep going.

When training rolls around on Tuesday, I'm more confident about my soccer skills, but less confident about having to face Ted and my teammates.

Just do it quickly! I tell myself. Like ripping off a Band-Aid.

The boys are sitting in a circle, getting their boots on, and Ted is standing next to them looking at his clipboard when I walk over. They all look up at me. I take a deep breath.

'I'm really sorry I lied to you all,' I say in a shaky voice. 'I was just really scared you wouldn't want me on your team. I didn't want to lose soccer, too, like I lost AFL. I'm sorry.'

The boys all smile. A few of them nod and Dylan gives me a discreet thumbs up. Ted smiles at me, too.

'You should have just told us you were a girl from the start, Sam,' he says gently. 'We're all about a mixed gender vibe here at the club. It would never have been an issue.'

'Yeah,' says Archie, smiling.

'Yeah, it's fine,' says Toby.

One by one the boys all nod, or mumble their agreement, and I slowly let out my breath in relief. Turns out I was worried about nothing. These boys totally would have accepted me from the start. The only one with the issue was me. It was all in my head! And if I wasn't sure before, I definitely am now that Chelsea was totally fibbing about her Uncle saying he didn't want girls on the team.

Noah grins. 'And we promise not to go easy on you just because you're a girl.'

I grin back. 'And I promise not to go easy on you lot, just because you're boys.'

Everyone laughs and Ted claps his hands loudly.

'Okay,' he says. 'Let's do some laps!'

As I take off alongside the rest of my team, I promise myself that I'll do everything I can to prove to them all that I deserve to be part of the Knights.

I'm not going to let them down.

CHAPTER SEVENTEEN

EAST FREMANTLE PRIMARY SCHOOL
ART ROOM
WEDNESDAY
2.10 PM

'That's looking fantastic, girls,' Miss Keystone says, leaning over our messy table.

I smile shyly. 'Thanks, Miss Keystone.'

Chelsea doesn't say a word. In fact, she hasn't said a thing through the whole class, which is very weird for her. The two of us have been sitting in stony silence as we put the finishing touches to our mosaic project. Mister Bottle Cap Frog is looking pretty awesome actually. I'm really proud of it and am trying to ignore the negative vibes coming from Chelsea's side of the table.

Chelsea has been even meaner than usual since I told her to 'blow it out her ear' on Monday, and has been whispering 'circus freak' and 'liar' whenever she walks past me. Yesterday in class, she drew a picture of me getting hit in the face with a soccer ball and stuck it on the back of my chair. I just don't understand how someone as nice as Ted can be related to someone as horrible as Chelsea.

'Keep it up,' Miss Keystone says, before moving on to the next table where Bobbi and Cam are making a tree out of egg cartons. It's got a bit of a lean to it and looks like it's going to topple over at any minute. Hopefully Miss Keystone can sort that out.

'I heard my mum talking to Uncle Ted last night,' Chelsea says suddenly.

She's smiling at me, which is a bad sign. A very bad sign.

'So?' I say, trying to sound less interested than I am.

Chelsea smiles. 'So . . . Mum asked him how the team was going, and your name came up.'

My cool 'I couldn't care less' expression

flies out of the art room window. I stare at Chelsea, wide-eyed.

'Mine? Why?'

'Uncle Ted said he wasn't sure you were a good fit for the team. Actually, I think the words he used were "not soccer material". Yeah, that's right.'

I narrow my eyes. 'You're lying.'

'Am I?' Chelsea shrugs. 'Or is he just waiting for you to stuff up again this week so he can chuck you off the team?'

'You mean the way you got kicked out?'

Chelsea's face clouds over. 'Who told you that?'

But before I can answer, Miss Keystone claps her hands to get our attention.

'Listen up, everyone,' she says loudly. 'I'm so impressed with your pieces that I've decided we're going to have an exhibition in the hall next Monday at lunchtime. I want the whole school to see how creative and talented the Grade Sixes are!'

Everyone claps and cheers, except me. I want to get as far away from Chelsea Flint as I can right now. I hop down off my stool and head for the bathroom.

⚽

Lying in bed, I can't stop thinking about what Chelsea said.

Is Ted really waiting to see if I can prove myself at Sunday's game? Chelsea is probably lying again, just like she did about Ted not wanting girls on the team. But what if she isn't? If Ted can keep his own family off his team, what's to stop him kicking out the new player if they're not up to scratch?

My stomach churns, and these questions swirl around my head so fast that I feel like a human washing machine. I'm already nervous about the game on Sunday and now I'm even more stressed. What if I stuff up the offside rule again? What if I don't remember what formation I'm supposed to stay in? All my extra practice might not make one bit of difference once I'm playing against another team. Two weeks ago, I wouldn't have cared if I never played soccer again, but now it's gotten under my skin and I want to prove that I'm 'soccer material'. Saturday might be my final match, and I don't like the idea of that at all.

But then I think about what Levi said about me needing to get out of my own head. I've been doing the extra practice this week and, if I keep doing it every week, I'm going to get better and better, just like I did with AFL. I need to push Chelsea's poisonous words out of my brain once and for all, and focus on my training.

In bed, I stare up at my David Beckham poster and decide right then and there that I'm not going to let what Chelsea said get to me. I like soccer now. I like it a lot and I'm going to get better at it, whatever it takes.

Penny gives a soft snore at the end of my bed and I nudge her gently with my foot. She wakes up, turns on her side and settles down again with a contented sigh.

I sigh and turn over, too, jealous of Penny and her uncomplicated doggy life.

CHAPTER EIGHTEEN

THE QUOKKAS' HOME GROUND
SATURDAY
2.45 pm

'Sam and Dylan, you're both off,' Ted says. 'The rest of you get out there and have fun.'

Dylan and I obediently sit down on the sideline to watch the first half of our game against the Quokkas, and shout, 'Go, Knights!' as loudly as we can every few minutes, but secretly I'm disappointed. For the first time since I joined the Knights, we have a full team, plus extra players, so I know someone has to start on the bench. I'd just hoped it wouldn't be me.

How am I going to show Ted how much I've improved if I'm stuck on the sidelines? To make things even worse, Mum and Dad are here today. It's an away game, so they insisted on driving me and staying to watch.

I jiggle my legs up and down and my hands twitch in my lap as the other team score their first goal. I'm itching to get out there now.

'Don't worry,' Dylan says, as if reading my mind. 'He'll put us on before the end of the half.'

But when the whistle blows for half-time, Dylan has been swapped out, but I'm still on the sideline. The score is 1–1. I'm standing quietly at the back while the others all drink greedily from their water bottles and slurp their orange quarters when Ted turns to me.

'Sam, you're in midfield,' he says. 'Remember to keep the triangle formation.'

I jump up and start stretching. I'm so ready to get out there! Mum and Dad give me an encouraging thumbs up from across the pitch.

'You good, Kerr?' Jack asks, as we walk out onto the pitch.

'Yep!' I say, sounding more confident than I feel.

The ref blows the whistle and the Quokkas take the kick-off. They're fast, faster than a lot of our boys, and their passing is amazing. The players stay in position and they know how to control the ball. Before we know it, they're up in the goal area and their striker is taking a shot. But Archie is ready, and he knocks it away just in time.

Dylan returns the ball to centre with a massive kick to Ky, who gets in a short pass to me. I tap the ball to control it, but my opponent is on me like mud on a boot, and he sweeps it out from under my foot, then shoots off with it in his possession.

Damn!

The Quokkas play a good game, but the Knights hold their own and Archie successfully blocks their next three attempts at goal. With only a couple of minutes left in the game, the score is still 1–1 and both teams are exhausted. It's been a tough match and I still haven't done anything that would make Ted want to keep me on the team.

Ky kicks the ball out so it's the Quokkas' throw in and they've got possession of the ball again. One of their players heads straight down the middle of the pitch. I take off after him, but Noah gets there before me and, with some excellent footwork, gets the ball back in his control and passes it to Archie.

'Get in there, Sam!' Ted calls from the sidelines.

'Go, Sammy!' I hear Mum shout.

I hover on the edges and, when a Quokkas player snatches the ball away from Archie, I pounce, beating him with a quick scissor step and getting possession.

It's mine! This is my chance and I have to take it. A feeling of total certainty comes over me, as well as a kind of calm. I know what I need to do with that ball right now.

All the doubts and fears and uncertainties seem to vanish into the cold morning air and my mind is suddenly clear. I'm going to take that ball and drive it down the field, all the way to that net.

I run towards the goal, controlling the ball with my feet the whole time. When I'm

in range, I pull my left foot back and, with every bit of strength I have, kick it square at the goal. The goalie tries to reach for it, but the ball shoots past him and straight into the left corner of the net.

GOAL!

The ref blows his whistle to signal the end of the game and everyone on the sidelines goes crazy, including Mum and Dad, who appear to be hugging complete strangers on either side of them.

Dylan runs towards me with his hands in the air and I'm so happy that, without thinking, I throw my body into a cartwheel, then flip over backwards in the air and land squarely on my feet.

'Woooo-hoooooo!' I yell.

A huge cheer goes up from the crowd, including the Quokkas supporters, and my beaming teammates all run towards me. As Dylan, Ky and Cooper hoist me up onto their shoulders, I hear a familiar voice shouting, 'Onya, Sammy!'

I look over to see Levi standing next to Ted, waving his hands and clapping like a lunatic. Indi, Daniel and Maddi are beside him, too, and they're all grinning from ear to ear. Mum and Dad have made their way around to join them, and seeing my family all standing together, clapping and cheering for me, is the best feeling in the whole world.

It looks like the Kerrs just might be a soccer family after all.

CHAPTER NINETEEN

It's Monday, two days after THE BEST GAME EVER, and me and my whole class spend all of recess setting up our recyclable art pieces around the hall for the exhibition. Instead of standing over here and helping me, Chelsea is on the other side of the hall whispering with Nikita and giving me strange sly looks. I'm trying to ignore her but it's not easy.

I'll probably never know if Chelsea was telling the truth about Ted wanting me off the team, but that's okay. After our win yesterday, Ted said I 'played really well' and to 'keep it up', so that's all I need to know.

'That's high praise from Ted,' Dylan had whispered to me after Ted had walked away.

I lift our mosaic out of the box and up onto the table, then step back to admire it. Mister Bottle Cap Frog turned out pretty well. Indi places her art piece next to mine. Her and Charlie have done an awesome job with their toilet roll bird feeder. I'd totally eat off it if I was a bird.

A disgusting smell suddenly hits my nostrils.

'What stinks?'

'It wasn't me!' Indi cries.

We turn to find Dylan standing behind us, holding his tin can windchime. Indi leans forward to sniff it, then jumps back.

'Poooh! What is that smell?'

'We used dog food tins,' Dylan says with a shrug.

'Did you wash them first?' I lift one tin up and look inside. 'Dylan, I can see bits of dog food still in there. *Gross!*'

'I know. I'm on my way to the sinks now,' Dylan says, grinning. 'Miss Keystone told me to go wash them out.'

We look over to see Miss Keystone glaring at Dylan, shaking her head in disbelief.

Seriously, what is he *like*!

'Dylan,' Miss Keystone calls out. 'Have you washed those tins yet?'

'Doing it now, Miss,' Dylan calls back, swinging the tins from side to side and releasing a fresh wave of dog food aroma into the air.

'Dylan! Gross!' Indi and I shout, holding our noses as we push a laughing Dylan towards the sinks.

We turn back to our pieces and Indi gives me a nudge.

'Hey, you're just like those bottle caps,' she says.

'Huh?'

She nods at Mister Bottle Cap Frog. 'I bet those caps never thought they'd be a frog one day, just like you never thought you'd be a soccer player. But here you both are.'

I nod and grin at Mister Frog. 'Yep, he's a pad-hopper and I'm a code-hopper! How cool is that?'

On our way to soccer training the next afternoon, Dylan and I walk alongside each other, arguing about the best player of 2004.

'It's definitely Beckham,' I say.

'No way!' Dylan exclaims. 'Ronaldo, for sure!'

I juggle the soccer ball between my feet and think about how weird it is that only a few short weeks ago I thought I'd never be happy again without AFL in my life. Now look at me! Who knew soccer could be so great?

I can't wait until our next game on Saturday. Ky has told me about a cool move that I'm busting to try. In fact, I might try it at training today. I'm so lost in these new and happy thoughts that I don't notice the new, fully kitted-out Knights player talking to Ted until Dylan and I join the rest of the team on the clubhouse steps. The new player has his back to us, with his hoodie pulled up over his head.

'Hey, everyone,' Ted says. 'We have a new player joining the Knights this week. This is . . .'

The new player turns around and I see that it's not a boy at all.

It's my worst nightmare.

'. . . my niece, Chelsea.'

Dylan and I snap our heads around to look at each other.

What?

Our shocked expressions suddenly crack, and we begin to laugh.

Ah well. I guess you can't have it all!

ABOUT THE AUTHOR

Sam Kerr is the captain of the Australian women's national soccer team – the Matildas – and a leading goal scorer for Chelsea in the English FA Women's Super League. She burst onto the W-League scene as a fifteen-year-old playing with Perth Glory. In 2016 she played for the Matildas at the Olympics in Brazil, and she was the top goal scorer in the 2017 Tournament of Nations. Since joining Chelsea in 2019, Sam has positioned herself as one of the best female strikers in the world. She was named 2018 Young Australian of the Year.

COMING SOON!

Available in print, eBook and eAudio
in December 2021.
Read on for a sneak peek!

CHAPTER ONE

'*Chelsea Flint* joined your soccer team?!'

Indi stops so suddenly that Dylan bumps straight into her.

'Um, hello?' he says, glaring at her.

But Indi keeps staring at me, eyes wide behind her blue-rimmed glasses.

It's Wednesday morning, and Indi, Dylan and I are walking to school together, like we do every day. Well, Dylan and Indi are walking. I'm gliding beside them on my skateboard. It's a sunny day in East Fremantle but with Chelsea now on our soccer team, it feels like a storm is coming.

She's East Fremantle Primary's biggest bully and in the six years we've been at school, I've only ever stood up to Chelsea once. That happened last week when I told her to 'Blow it out her ear' in front of the whole school. She's won't forget about what I said anytime soon. No one embarrasses Chelsea Flint and gets away with it.

When Chelsea rocked up to training yesterday and our coach Ted told us she was joining our team, Dylan and I laughed and joked about it. But when I woke up this morning the terrible truth hit me like a tonne of bricks. It feels like a bad dream. Actually, it feels more like a nightmare. The kind where you wake up screaming, fall on the floor and scare the life out of your dog who's sleeping on your bed.

'What a nightmare,' Indi says now.

I stare at my best friend in amazement. Did she just read my mind? Actually, yeah, she probably did. Best friends can do that sometimes.

'Maybe Chelsea will get bored and quit?' Indi adds hopefully, starting to walk towards school again.

'I don't think so,' Dylan says. 'She was having fun last night, and she's a good player too.'

I almost skate straight into a tree.

'You thought she was *good*?'

Dylan looks like he wants to hide behind the nearest bush. Not an easy thing to do when you're a five-foot-eight-inches tall eleven-year-old.

'I dunno . . . she wasn't terrible,' he shrugs.

Has Dylan lost his mind? Why is he sticking up for Chelsea Flint? If anyone has the right to bag her out it's Dylan. Chelsea is meaner to him than anyone else at school. Most people would think that a five-foot-eight-inches tall boy wouldn't be scared of a tiny blonde girl with a big mouth, but they'd be wrong. Dylan is super shy and awkward. But he's honest too, so if he reckons Chelsea is a good player, it must be true.

This fact only makes me feel worse.

Indi puts her arm around me — an awkward thing to do when I'm rolling along on a skateboard.

'It'll be fine,' she says reassuringly. 'Chelsea can't be mean to you at soccer. She'll be on her best behaviour in front of her uncle!'

Oh yeah, I forgot to say. Ted, our coach, is Chelsea's uncle. But I wouldn't say that she'd be on her best behaviour for him. She's *never* on her best behaviour.

Urg. I'd *finally* started to feel good about playing with the Knights. I even kicked my first goal last Sunday.

Yep. Life was good . . . and then Chelsea Flint had to go and spoil everything!